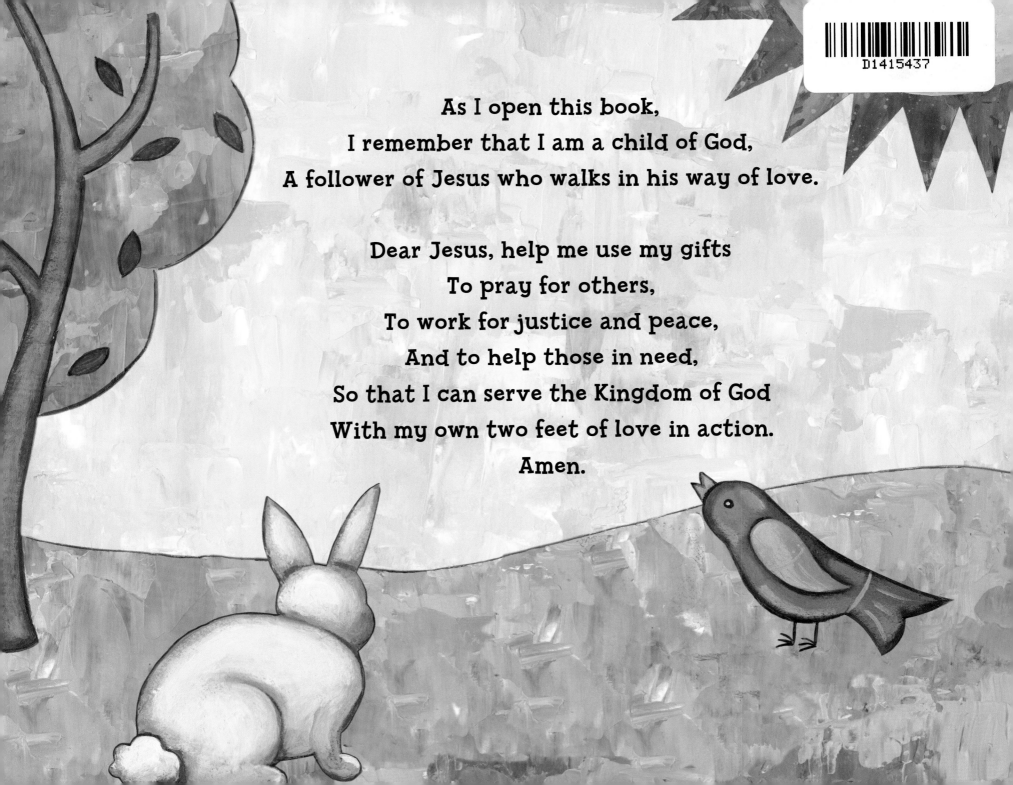

As I open this book,
I remember that I am a child of God,
A follower of Jesus who walks in his way of love.

Dear Jesus, help me use my gifts
To pray for others,
To work for justice and peace,
And to help those in need,
So that I can serve the Kingdom of God
With my own two feet of love in action.
Amen.

Philip loved life
on Green Street.

It had sidewalks for skating.

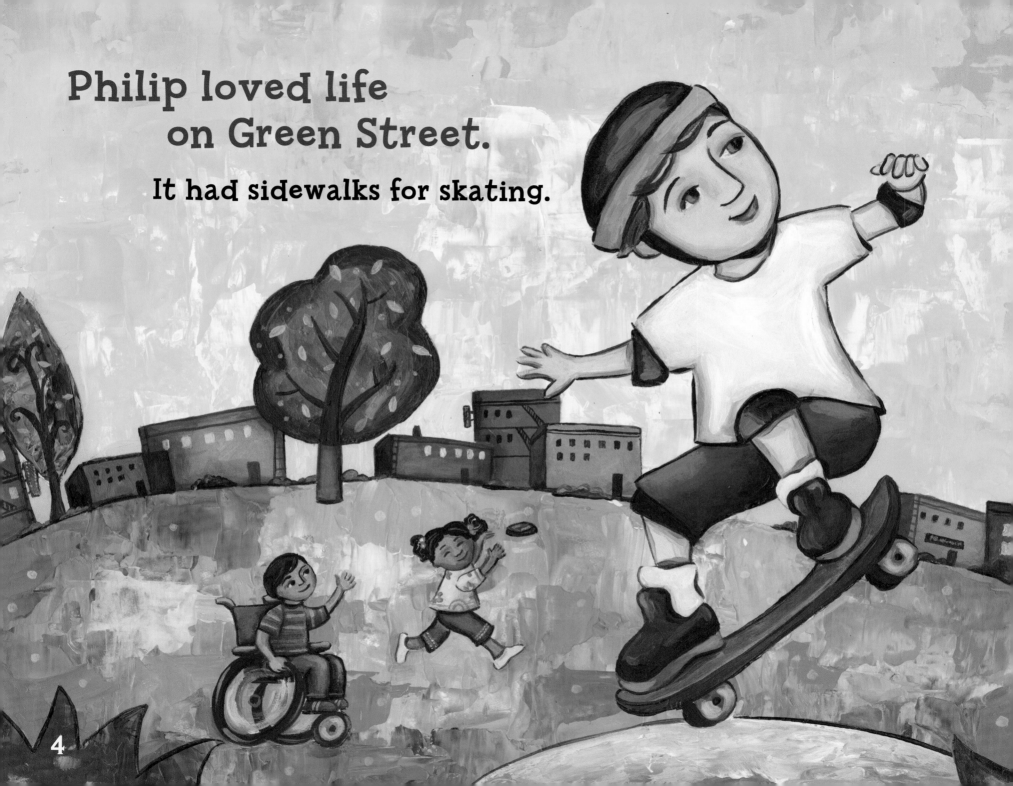

4

Green Street Park

United States Conference
of Catholic Bishops

Department of Justice,
Peace, and Human Development

In Partnership with Loyola Press

Illustrated by Jill Arena

LOYOLA PRESS.
A JESUIT MINISTRY

LOYOLA PRESS.
A JESUIT MINISTRY

3441 N. Ashland Avenue
Chicago, Illinois 60657
(800) 621-1008
www.loyolapress.com

Author: United States Conference of Catholic Bishops;
Department of Justice, Peace, and Human Development

Contributing Editor: Susan Blackaby

Cover design: Jill Arena

Illustrations: Jill Arena

ISBN-13: 978-0-8294-4099-7

ISBN-10: 0-8294-4099-2

Library of Congress Control Number: 2015930435

Printed in the United States of America

15 16 17 18 19 20 Bang 10 9 8 7 6 5 4 3 2 1

It had a park for shooting hoops.

It had lots of kids to play with.

5

At night, Philip said his prayers. He always ended the same way. "Bless my family. Bless my friends.

6

And thank you, God,
    for Green Street.

Amen."

7

Philip met Sara and Marcus at the park.
Marcus passed the ball to Sara.
"Let's play H-O-R-S-E," he said,
"You can start." Sara made the first shot.
Then Marcus took a turn. He missed.

The ball sailed past Philip.

It landed in the dirt and rolled into a thick patch of prickly weeds. "I'll get it," said Philip.

Philip stepped through the brush.
He hopped over an old tire.
He went around an old fence.
He reached into the weeds
and picked up the ball.

"St. Francis
should see our old park," said Philip.
Sara nodded. Marcus laughed.

Sister Mary Clare looked at them. "What do you mean?"
"The Green Street Park is a mess," said Philip.
"It needs to get fixed up. St. Francis would take care of it."
Sister Mary Clare smiled.

"Maybe you can try
to be more like him."

On Saturday, Philip took garden tools
and trash bags to the park.
He dragged the tire to the big trash bin.
He pulled weeds. He worked all morning.
But when he looked around,
there still was lots of work to do.
Philip felt bad.

"I can't do this by myself. I need help."

At home, Philip asked his family what he could do.

"I think the park needs to be fixed up."

"Could we add a big garden? What would the mayor say?" continued Philip.
"Come up with a plan," said Mom.
"Then ask the mayor what he thinks."

17

Philip got the kids on Green Street to help.

The kids made drawings of the park.
They showed how nice it could be.
Sara drew a flower bed.

Marcus drew a birdbath.
Birds splashed in the water.
Philip drew a vegetable patch.

It had a big vine of green peas.

The parents helped, too.
Sara's mom made a list of supplies.
Marcus's dad added up the costs.
Philip's dad made a map.

Philip's mom typed the letter.

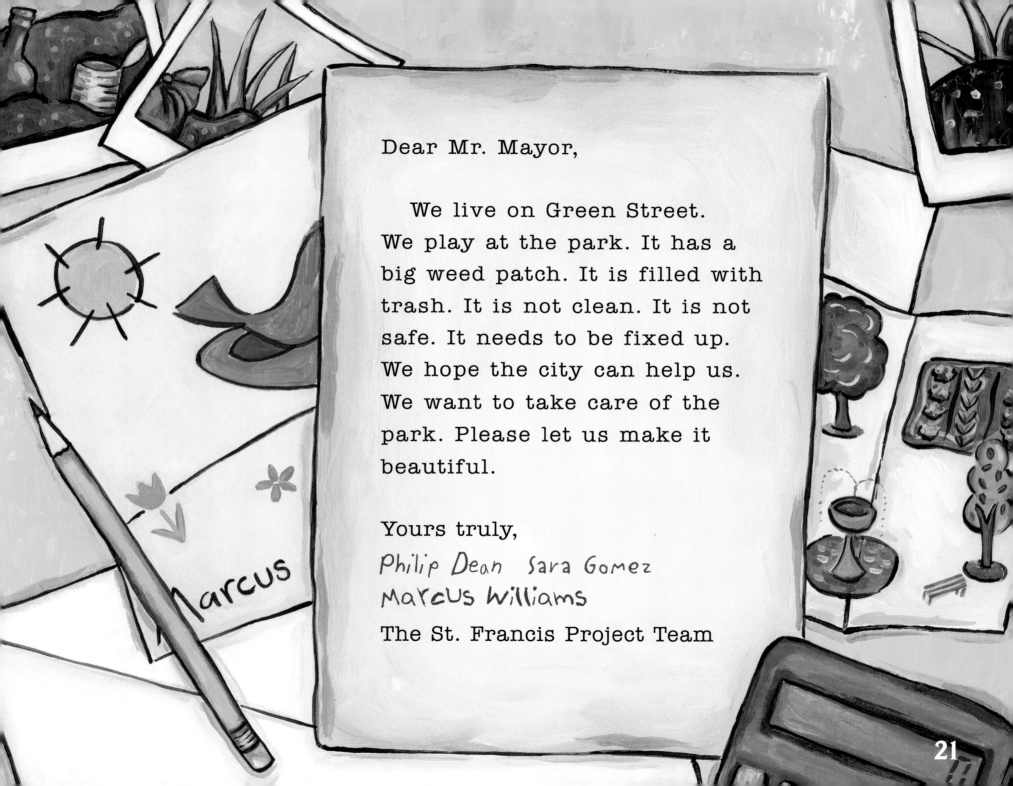

Dear Mr. Mayor,

   We live on Green Street. We play at the park. It has a big weed patch. It is filled with trash. It is not clean. It is not safe. It needs to be fixed up. We hope the city can help us. We want to take care of the park. Please let us make it beautiful.

Yours truly,
Philip Dean   Sara Gomez
Marcus Williams
The St. Francis Project Team

The kids sent the mayor
the drawings and notes.

The mayor
sent a letter back.

22

One day, everyone on Green Street met at the park.
A city crew helped them clear the lot.
They took away the trash. They brought in new soil.

In just a few weeks, the garden was ready.

Mayor Lee came to help plant the flower beds.

So did Sister Mary Clare.

Now the kids meet at the park to play.
But first they pull weeds before they play W-E-E-D-S.
They make sure the plants have water.

They pick the vegetables.

The families on Green Street get all the vegetables they need.
The leftover vegetables go to the soup kitchen

at the church.

At night, Philip says his prayers. And he always ends them the same way.

"Bless my family. Bless my friends. And thank you, God, for green peas. They are my favorite. **Amen.**"

Talk About It

After reading the book, discuss the following questions.

1 What was wrong with Green Street Park? What did Philip do first to try to solve the problem? Did it work?

2 What did Philip and his friends do to get the help they needed to fix the park?

3 How do you think the children felt after the park was fixed? What makes you think so?

4 Why is it important to take care of God's creation?

5 How might you help care for God's creation in your own community?

Possible Answers

1. The park was full of weeds and garbage. He tried to pull the weeds and clean up the garbage. He couldn't do it all by himself.

2. Philip talked to his mother, he and his friends made plans, and they contacted the mayor to get the help they needed. They also invited their neighbors on Green Street to help them.

3. I think the children felt proud and happy. They are smiling as they work on the park and as they enjoy it after it is fixed.

4. It is important to take care of God's creation because as his children, we have a responsibility to protect it.

5. Answers will vary.

Put **Two Feet** of **Love** *in Action*

Each storybook includes discussion questions and blackline masters for catechists, teachers, and parents to help share the following teachings of the Church in ways that children can readily understand:

- We are called to practice **social justice** and work for foundational change.
- We are called to perform **charitable works** and help others in need.

Visit **www.loyolapress.com/twofeetoflove** to access these teaching materials.

Additionally, a Pray Me a Story reflection guide is available. This guide uses the book as a springboard for entering into imaginative prayer. After hearing the story, the child is gently guided into the scene to meet Jesus and prayerfully speak to him as one friend speaks to another.

The
Two Feet of Love
in Action

SOCIAL JUSTICE

CHARITABLE WORKS

As disciples of Jesus, we must put two feet of love in action!

We walk with the Charitable Works "foot" when we help make a situation better in the short term, such as picking up trash in a park.

We walk with the Social Justice "foot" when we help make a permanent difference, such as asking the mayor to help fix the park and inviting our neighbors to build a community garden.

How can you put two feet of love in action?

Visit the website of the U.S. Catholic bishops for more on the Two Feet of Love in Action.